"It's Easter morning! Here are your
Easter baskets."

"There is one more basket. It's moving!
It is a baby Easter bunny!"

"Come outside for our Easter egg hunt.
There are Easter eggs all over the yard."

"Look! The Easter bunny is hunting for eggs, too."

"We found a lot of eggs. But the Easter bunny is looking for something better—other Easter babies!"

"Here are some baby chipmunks! Many babies are born in the spring, just like baby Easter bunnies."

"Here are more babies—tiny baby field mice."

"Will the Easter bunny find even more babies? Baby robins are chirping for a nice, juicy worm."

"Don't worry, Easter bunny, that's just a baby turtle."

"Look! The Easter bunny wants to explore.
Let's follow him."

"Wait, little bunny! Here is another baby—
a kitten. The mother cat is coming to find it."

"The Easter bunny is hopping into the woods. Will it find babies there, too?

"Here is a baby deer—a fawn! It is hiding while the mother is nearby."

"The Easter bunny is going to Farmer Ben's farm. There are sure to be babies here, like this mother horse and her baby foal."

"Hello, Farmer Ben! We are looking for spring babies."

"Then take a look at this brand-new calf. Isn't he a beauty?"

"If you want to see babies, just step this way. These are my favorite Easter babies—chicks and ducklings!"